Now here's a story for you,
full of such fun and exciting stuff
you will surely love it.
And the best part is . . . it's all true.

The

1 2 3 GO!

to Alvie and Bumpy Bumpy [B.I.]
Big thanks to Daniel and David

RUN

DIN

AWAY
NER

CANDLEWICK PRESS
CAMBRIDGE, MASSACHUSETTS

Allan Ahlberg and Bruce Ingman

There was once a boy.

Banjo, his name was, yes, Banjo Cannon.

Well, he was a little boy, this boy,

lived in a house,

slept in a bed,

wore all the usual sorts of clothes,

socks and scarves and such,

loved his cat, named Mildred,

and his mom and dad, named Mr. and Mrs.

and every day,

summer or winter, rain or shine,

had a sausage for his dinner . . .

on his own little plate,
with his own little knife and fork
and salt shaker and ketchup,
at his own little table,
with his own little chair.

Yes, a sausage, a sausage for his dinner.

Now here's the exciting part,
the unbelievable part—though it is all true.

One sunny summer's day,

just as Banjo,

with his knife in one hand and his fork in the other,

was leaning forward and smiling happily

at the thought of eating his dinner,

the sausage—Melvin, his name was—

jumped, yes, jumped, right up off the plate . . .

and ran away.

Well then, of course, as you might expect,
the fork ran after the sausage,
the knife ran after the fork,
the plate ran after the knife,
the little table and the little chair ran after the plate,

and Banjo, that hungry little boy, ran after all of them.

Actually, if you want the whole truth,
he ran after a few others as well.
You see, Banjo did not only have
a sausage on his plate.
That would be silly, wouldn't it?
Just a sausage, one measly little sausage,
for a hungry boy's dinner.

No, Banjo also had:
three fat peas,
four baby carrots,
and a handful of fries.

Yes, and the thing is, of course, they were all on the plate as well.
And when Melvin ran off, they, as you might expect, followed him.

The peas, as it happened, were all boys: Peter, Percival, and Paul.
And the carrots, all girls: Caroline, Clara, Camilla, and Christabel.

As for the fries,
well, there really were too many to name all of them,
though being French, of course,
they had names like François, Fifi, and so forth.

So that's it, the absolute truth, the complete picture—see?
Here they are, the whole lot of them, not forgetting Mildred the cat
and Mr. and Mrs., and Bruce, the next-door neighbor's dog—
nearly *did* forget him, though he was chasing Mildred, actually—
all racing down the road.

Well, the first thing that happened was the carrots, all four of them, escaped by hiding in a paper bag,

Bruce chased Mildred up a tree,

and a pigeon ate Percival.

Melvin, meanwhile, was running strongly on his two little legs.

He came to a crosswalk, waited for the walk light, crossed the road, and ran into the park.

The next thing that happened was
Mr. and Mrs. bought three ice creams,
a couple of the French fries escaped
by sailing away in a toy boat:
"Au revoir!"
"Bon voyage!"
"Hourra!"

and a duck ate Paul.

Banjo, meanwhile,
was running strongly
on *his* two little legs,
and the chair and the table
were both running strongly
on their four little legs.

Actually, that's not entirely true.
The little chair in particular was
quite out of breath.
He had to stop and rest for a while.
Only then an old lady came along and sat on him.
She was out of breath too.
So then, of course, the little chair was stuck there for a time.

Melvin, meanwhile, was still racing away,

with the knife and fork close behind, and the little plate,

and Mr. and Mrs. . . . and so forth.

Presently, a picnicking family spotted the fork,
and the knife, too, and grabbed them.
At the same time, a boiled egg named Billy
saw what was going on
and, in the confusion, ran off himself.

A couple of little girls
who were skipping on the grass
spotted the plate and grabbed her—
she was a girl plate—Saskia, her name was—
and started using her as a Frisbee.
Which, as it turned out,
"Wheeee!"
the little plate much enjoyed.

Well now, there was a pond in the park,
that's where the toy boat was sailing,
and Melvin ran around it.
And there was a baseball field,
and Melvin ran around that.

The rest of the French fries stopped here
and sat down to watch the baseball game, actually,
and nobody noticed them.

By this time, the sunny summer's day was coming to an end
and almost everybody was out of breath.
Melvin, that sturdy little sausage,

slowed to a stroll,

to a dawdle,

and, finally, stopped altogether.
Whereupon, along came Banjo, that hungry little boy,

and, oh dear . . .

ate

him.

Well, nearly.

He would have done, he really would.

Only just then along came

his hot and bothered poor old mom.

"No, no!" she cried. "Don't eat that,"

meaning Melvin.

"Don't eat that,
it's been
on the ground!"

The next thing that happened was
Melvin seized his chance,
ran off again, and hid in the long grass,
where, as it turned out, at that very moment,
the baseball—named Marlon—
was also hiding.

Meanwhile,
the athletic little table,
urged on by the salt shaker
and ketchup, was still racing along.
His style was much admired
by a number of park benches.
On the other hand, Peter, the last of the peas—
remember him?—
had well and truly disappeared.
It was a mystery.

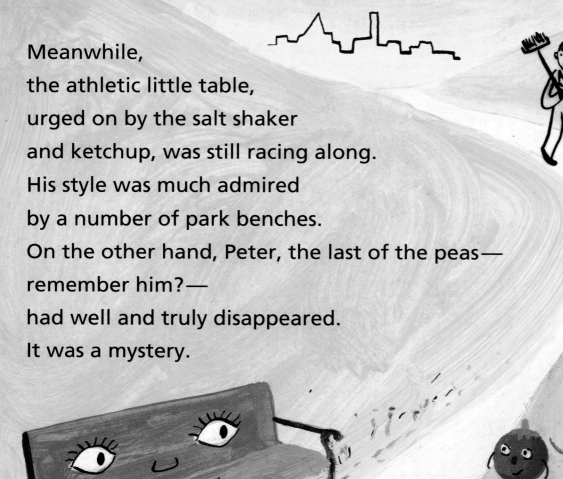

He had to be
there somewhere.
Yes, take a look if you like.
See if you can spot him.

It was a sunny
summer's evening.
Home went Banjo,
carried high on the shoulders
of his poor old dad
and his poor old mom.
Bruce, the next-door neighbor's dog,
went home too . . .
and down the tree came Mildred.

So there we are—that's the story.

Full of such fun, don't you agree?

And exciting stuff . . . yes.

Of course, poor little Banjo is still hungry.

Hungrier than ever, in fact.

Luckily, help is at hand.

You see, every day (or evening),

rain or shine, summer or winter,

after his dinner Banjo has a plum pie for his dessert.

In his own little bowl,
with his own little spoon,
and his own little pitcher of cream.
Yes, a plum pie, a plum pie—
named Joyce on this particular occasion—
for his dessert.

So that's all right . . .

isn't it?

Text copyright © 2006 by Allan Ahlberg
Illustrations copyright © 2006 by Bruce Ingman

First U.S. paperback edition 2008

Library of Congress Cataloging-in-Publication Data is available.
Library of Congress Catalog Card Number 2005058126
ISBN 978-0-7636-3142-0 (hardcover)
ISBN 978-0-7636-3893-1 (paperback)

2 4 6 8 10 9 7 5 3 1

Printed in Singapore

This book was typeset in Frutiger.
The illustrations were done in acrylic.

Candlewick Press
2067 Massachusetts Avenue
Cambridge, Massachusetts 02140

visit us at www.candlewick.com